The Knife Thrower

'The prose is beautiful and meticulously crafted, yet always summoning what is just beyond the power of words . . . Millhauser is a master storyteller' *Time Out*

'Millhauser's forte is finding new ways of dramatising the American Dream as it turns, so often and so easily, into a kind of waking nightmare . . . Clever and intriguing'

Literary Review

'While these stories are arrestingly original, they also have an ageless mythic quality. Written with deadpan accuracy and fastidious detachment, they are unforgettable'

Harper's & Queen

'As sinister as it is fanciful . . . [*The Knife Thrower*] is Millhauser at his purest' *San Francisco Chronicle*

'Millhauser draws us effortlessly into the shimmering worlds of his fictions. His writing has a rare quality that is hard to resist' *Boston Globe*

'Curious and tantalising . . . Millhauser's own ingenuity is delicious . . . The strength and glitter of its imaginative grip lies in Millhauser's ability to weave detail into detail, the lovingly real and possible into the extravagantly impossible'

A. S. Byatt, *Washington Post*

'Splendid flashes of absurdity and satire. Millhauser has a rich, sly sense of humour . . . in his exploration of the complicated response we have to the products and projections of our own minds, Millhauser is without equal among contemporary writers' *New York Times Book Review*

Steven Millhauser was born in New York City and grew up in Connecticut. His stories have appeared in various publications including the *New Yorker* and *Esquire*. His most recent novel, *Martin Dressler*, was the winner of the 1997 Pulitzer Prize for Fiction and was also shortlisted for the US National Book Award. Steven Millhauser teaches at Skidmore College and lives with his wife and two children in Saratoga Springs, New York.

BY THE SAME AUTHOR

Martin Dressler: The Tale of an American Dreamer
The Barnum Museum
From the Realm of Morpheus
In the Penny Arcade
Little Kingdoms
Portrait of a Romantic
Edwin Mullhouse: The Life and Death of an American Writer